MW01204663

Hermann Shadows

Ghosts in the Heart of Wine Country

Happy Hauntings!

Dan

Dan Terry

edited by Glen and Sue Blesi

Hermann Shadows

Copyright 2009 Missouri Kid Press

Cover Photo by Dan Terry
View of Hermann City Cemetery

ISBN13: 978-0-9797654-5-2
ISBN: 0-9797654-5-5

Missouri Kid Press
P. O. Box 111
Stanton, Missouri 63079

Table of Contents

About the Author

Dan Terry is a native of Franklin County, Missouri. He attended school in Stanton and Sullivan, where he participated in public speaking competitions, advancing to state level. He graduated in 1981.

Like many young people in the community, Dan worked as a guide at Meramec Caverns, where he developed an interest in history.

After a four-year hitch in the United States Coast Guard, he began a career in law enforcement, almost as an accident. In 1995, Terry went to work for the New Haven Police Department and was promoted to Assistant Chief of Police in 2006.

Even in his childhood, Dan was fascinated with the paranormal, mostly through such television shows as the *Twilight Zone, Night Gallery,* and *Kolchack: The Night Stalker.*

When Dan was old enough to drive and managed to get a car, he began investigating local haunted places with a small group of friends. During his Coast Guard days, he continued to go to alleged haunted places, using the old 1970's ghost-hunting style of stalking the ghost rather than interacting with it.

After concentrating on his career and family for many years, Dan was able to return to ghost hunting after the children were grown. He visited many haunted places and, with the help of Misouri Paranormal Research members, learned new procedures, such as how to get EVP's and paranormal photography. He is now known as "The Spookstalker". Dan has investigated homes and businesses from Wilmington, North Carolina to Cimmeron, New Mexico, including a very haunted museum in Wichita, Kansas, and the Crescent Hotel in Eureka Springs, Arkansas. He was one of the early investigators of the Waverly Hills Sanitarium in Louisville, Kentucky.

After writing a newspaper article for the *New Haven Leader* about local haunted spots in 2005, Dan began writing for *Haunted*

Times Magazine and soon became a regular contributor. In 2007, his first book, *Beyond the Shadows: Exploring the Ghosts of Franklin County*, was published. In 2008, it was followed by *Missouri Shadows: A Journey Through the Lesser Known, the Famous and the Infamous Haunts of Missouri*. He has also been published in police-related magazines.

His published articles include an interview with Lt. Col. Jesse Marcel, Jr., the last man acknowledged to have touched the debris from the 1947 Roswell crash, and other articles about Roswell and ghost hunting.

In addition, Dan recently served as the narrator/historian for a video entitled, *The Morse Mill Project,* and is scheduled to be part of a video about haunted places along the Missouri River.

He has spoken at several ghost conferences, including one at Ohio State Reformatory, and at the Mineral Springs Hotel and Spa at Alton, Illinois. In March 2009, Dan hosted the first ghost conference ever held in Franklin County, Missouri, and is planning a second conference in April 2010.

Dan Terry makes his home in New Haven, Missouri, a few miles east of Hermann, with his wife, Sherri.

Sue Blesi, Publisher

Foreword

I am sitting near the top of a bluff in Hermann, Missouri. Behind me is the piece of rock that gives "Stone Hill" its name. Below, a vineyard, and sound travel a very long way. The distant wail of a train, a single barking dog, the shouts of children playing baseball. I can easily imagine a steam calliope down the river, shouts of cargo unloading at long-gone docks, and perhaps, sadly, the explosion of an overheated boiler and the general chaos of disaster.

Sound travels here and spirits travel here. Perhaps these two energies follow the same paths.

In an almost mystical way, Hermann is protected by substantial hills on three sides and a pleasant bend in the river on the remaining side. It is a comfortable place for all residents – both living and dead. Only the silent, sleepy, houses can tell all that has lain hidden since the early days, and they may or may not talk to us. Some people say that things and places have souls, and there are others who say they do not. For myself, I cannot say.

Over the years, thousands of people were born here and lived normal, happy mundane lives. Hermann, Missouri, can easily trace its heritage back to 9 C.E. The area is very attractive and beyond a doubt, Native Americans, casual travelers and other adventurous visitors have seen this place, stopped here, stayed here, and on occasion, died here. I can understand how someone who is comfortable and content would choose to stay in Hermann well into the afterlife.

Sometimes I believe that this "less material" life is our true life, and that our vain presence on earth is the secondary or virtual phenomenon. I am not in any sense childishly superstitious, but scientific study and reflection have taught me that the known universe embraces the merest fraction of the whole. An overwhelming preponderance of evidence from numerous sources point to the existence of forces of great power and, so far as the human point of view is concerned, mystery.

Curious people know there is no sharp distinction between the real and the unreal.

However, who is to say any of this is "unreal." The stories are numerous and the evidence undeniable.

Dan is a meticulous researcher and an entertaining story teller. Together, let's explore a few of the ghosts in Hermann, Missouri, another of those wonderful, intriguing, haunted places. People, spirits and even a few well-loved pets. Perhaps we can shake some of those stories, and a few of the remaining souls, from their hiding places.

Michael Henry, Ph.D.
Founder, Downtown St. Charles Ghost Tours
August 2009

Introduction
WELCOME TO MY WORLD

I live in darkness.

My interest in ghost hunting started with my father, who said he didn't believe in ghosts, yet always had family stories to share about strange lights, images and missing or floating objects. It became a passion after I first watched *Kolchak: The Night Stalker,* a television show about a reporter who investigated the supernatural in 1974.

The U.S. military in the mid 80's was not a place to express an interest in the paranormal. After I was discharged, I became a police officer and had a family, further pushing my love for the strange to the background. Still, I continued to read books by Hans Holzer, Father Malachi Martin, Richard Winer and others. UFOs, ghosts, Yeti, anything I could find on the subject of the paranormal.

About the time the kids were grown, TV's *Ghost Hunters* brought paranormal investigation into the mainstream. I started again, and found my old ways of ghost hunting had become obsolete. Fortunately, Greg Myers and Steven LaChance of Missouri Paranormal Research took me by the hand and taught me new methods of obtaining evidence.

When you read these pages, several names will appear over and over again. Let me take this moment to introduce you to the cast of characters:

Steven LaChance, an extreme haunting survivor whose story has been featured on the Discovery Channel series, *A Haunting.* LaChance is a radio show host, public speaker, executive producer and director of the DVD feature, *The Morse Mill Project,* and recently published his first book about his experiences in the Union Screaming House, entitled *The Uninvited.* Steven has been invaluable in teaching me as well as helping with some of the stickier cases, including my only (to date) demonic one.

Tim Clifton, a former firefighter and photography expert, is truly a gifted sensitive along with being a modest man. He's been with me on several cases, and one fact I can verify is that if Tim says there is a ghost in the room, the evidence will surface.

Theresa Reavey is another who has been involved in more than her fair share of demonic cases, and approaches each one with courage and faith. Theresa can be depended on to assist and detect spirits, and her lavish use of Holy Water is legendary.

Sherri Terry, my wife and partner, is braver than I am and always there to put the brakes on my overactive imagination.

Two of the tools I use in many of the cases are listed below, along with a brief explanation.

1. The Ovilus: an electronic device that takes readings of electromagnetic energy, temperature, and pressure, then assigns a numerical value to the result, pulling a matching word from its internal dictionary. With time, a spirit can learn to speak through the machine. Strangely, words often come from the speakers that do not exist in the dictionary.

2. KII Meter: An EMF detector that lights up if a spirit gets close. Again, a spirit can answer simple yes and no questions by making the meter go off.

In these pages, you'll read stories that are unbelievable. In a couple of the situations, even though I was there, I still can't believe what happened. However, I can verify for you that each is the truth, the whole truth, and nothing but the truth.

The veil is thinning, and things are changing. Whether it is due to more people paying attention to the paranormal, thanks to TV's *Ghost Hunters* and other shows, or because of the rapidly-approaching end of the world in the year 2012, (as prophesized by the ancient Mayans and brought to the national stage in specials by the History Channel and an upcoming major motion picture), the spirits seem to want more attention.

After this, you'll know how to give that attention to them.

Acknowledgements

Over the years, I have tried to get ghost stories from the Hermann area. Finally, this year, it opened up for me in a most dramatic way.

I have to thank Lynn and Kecia from Lyndee's restaurant, who were the first to talk to me about their ghosts. That story was included in *Missouri Shadows,* and an updated version is in this book.

Tracy Mueller overheard a friend speak of the ghost in their bed and breakfast, and not only brought my name up to them but then contacted Sherri and I about it. We really owe her the debt for us getting the start there.

Jeanie Schultz, co-manager of the Wine Valley Inn, is the person I credit with starting the Hermann landslide of stories. Allowing us to investigate and write about her place, along with the Heidelberg, really opened Hermann for us. A special thanks to Jeanie.

Gary and Phyllis Craig, owners of the Zimmer Mit Fruhstuck Bed and Breakfast, also opened up their hearts and stories for me. Gary also arranged for me to meet Rebecca and Richard Ruediger, who graciously gave Sherri and me a tour of their beautiful home and the stories to go with it.

Ted and Deb Prusinowski have been great assets, as well providing material for a good chapter in this book. Both are well on their way to being top notch paranormal investigators, and I am pleased to invite them on my ghost hunts.

A special thank you goes to the ladies at the Gasconade County Historical Society, who have been a great help with my research.

Finally, let me give credit to the people who help to make this hobby of mine possible. My wife Sherri, who is with me on every ghost hunt; Steven LaChance, who turned a negative haunting he suffered through into a positive life lesson; Tim Clifton and Theresa Reavey, psychics I can call on for help at any time; Greg Myers from the Paranormal Task Force for teaching me so much a few years ago, Jacqui Carpenter, psychic and founder of IPRA for including me on the Morse Mill Project and other future collaborations, and Dr. Michael Henry, founder of the Mid-American Paranormal Society and the Downtown St. Charles Ghost Tours for his advice and assistance.

I am proud to say that, unlike many in the world of paranormal investigation, I can turn to these fine people for friendship and guidence. My only hope is the rest of the ghost hunting groups can follow that lead, and get along rather than attempt to tear down others out of jealousy, fear or simply the love of stirring the crap.

May all your spirits be bottled and bonded.

Behind every man now alive stands 30 ghosts, for that is the ratio by which the dead outnumber the living.
　　　　　　　　　—Arthur C. Clark, *2001: A Space Odyssey*

Paranormal Investigators

how do we choose?

Why do we do this?
Next to asking how I got into supernatural investigating, this is the most frequent question I hear. The best answer I've heard so far came from Sam Tyree of Great Plains Paranormal Investigations in Wichita, Kansas. In an interview, he referred to death as, "the next great horizon", and compared our desire to see what is on the other side to ancient sailors who risked their lives to see what was beyond the known ocean.

It's poetic. Man has always had a degree of awe concerning death. The ancient Egyptians built huge temples and buried their leaders with everything they thought they would need in the next world. In the Pacific islands, natives of the Vanuatu tribe took the bodies of the important men of the village out to the jungle and drained them of blood while an expert made effigies of them. The heads were removed from the corpses, and faces of the deceased were reconstructed from resin and placed over the skulls, which were believed to hold the spirits of the warriors. Bamboo bodies were affixed and decorated in a manner befitting their place in the village. The deceased then became guests of honor at a great feast. The effigies were then placed in a house for 20 years while the spirit slowly moved on to the next world.

All but the most devout religious people fear death. The one thing I have learned from ghost hunting that stands out above all others is the absolute knowledge that there is something on the other side. What is there, I cannot say. Is there a long, white tunnel, ending in a line of people with a small man passing out harps and haloes? Or, if you prefer, horns and pitchforks? A spiritual waiting room filled with souls eager for judgment? Golden streets and a saint to greet you? Again, I don't know what awaits us on the other side. Whatever it is, some don't go. I suspect some are afraid of judgment, being raised believing that they will spend an eternity on fire and in pain for the evil they've done. Some are just happy where they are, and to them, home is heaven. And I believe some don't even know they are dead, and are continuing with their daily lives, wondering why the strangers in their house will not speak with them. Unlike many, I do not believe that demonic spirits are everywhere. In fact, I would bet that true demonic cases are few and far between. In the years I've done this, I have encountered only one I believe was true evil.

So, when you're looking for a paranormal investigator, how do you choose? First, realize that there are charlatans, or supernatural con men out there. If they ask for money, they are probably only in it for that. I once heard of a woman who called a well-known paranormal talk show and explained that she was having what we would call an extreme haunting, and she contacted a local group for help. They charged her $300 to come in. After some hocus-pocus psychic readings, she was informed that one article of her extensive antique collection had a demon attached to it. They could not tell which object, but for another $400, they could take the entire collection and bury it on holy ground, thus stopping her problem. She paid the money, lost her very valuable collection of antiques, and the haunting continued. And, she asked, "What did she do wrong?" No group that I have ever met or worked with has ever charged to come in and investigate. That's what we are here for.

Since we can't find Bill Murray and Dan Aykroyd wearing their Ghostbuster clothes on a TV commercial telling you they're "Ready to believe you!", how do you find help? What are you looking for?

While some groups use scientific equipment and some use only psychics, neither is completely right or wrong. I tend to use both. But any group you choose should do a background investigation of the property, looking for deaths, accidents, or other reasons for ghostly activity. They will ask a lot of questions. Be wary of the ones who have already made up their minds before arriving on the scene of the investigation. In his book, *The Uninvited*, Steven LaChance discusses the group that came in to assist the family that lived in the Union Screaming House after he left. They immediately went to the teenage daughter's bedroom, declared by psychic telegraph that she was into witchcraft (she was not), and refused to consider any other possibility. THE PSYCHIC HAD SPOKEN!

Recently, I came to the conclusion that many psychics don't like my Ovilus or the KII meter. I was a guest at an investigation in which, every time the psychic leader asked the spirit to do something to show its presence, my KII meter would go crazy. I told him about it, and the guide made some remark about how interesting that was and continued on. But still, each time he asked for proof of the presence, the meter went to red or flashed crazily. Again I informed the guide, who was non-committal. However, when someone said "I feel cold", the psychic became very excited, telling everyone there was a cold spot.

My theory is that some psychics hate the machines because they take away from their being "special". After all, what good is it to have second sight and to speak for the spirit, if any clown like me with a $200 toy can give you the ghost's bloody phone number? We normal people no longer need the psychic to sense the presence when we can see the gauge on the meter swing wildly when the ghost is near.

The important thing to remember when you're confronted by spirit activity is that you are not alone. There are several reputable groups in the St. Louis area that can help you. And I may be contacted through my web site, www.spookstalker.com, if you have any questions. You may also seek out Dr. Michael Henry of MAPS, who is based in St. Charles, or Steven LaChance in Union. Another excellent choice is the very experienced Greg Myers of the Paranormal Task Force. Betsy Belanger, who runs tours of the Lemp Mansion in St. Louis, has been helping people with their paranormal problems for years. Supernatural Investigations, out of St. Louis, uses both scientific methods and psychics to assist people in dealing with the spirits in their homes.

There are several web sites listed at the end of this book where you can find help. Again, remember that you're not alone.

Hermann Shadows

This statue of Hermann faces the river at the corner of Highway 100 and Highway 19 behind the old city hall and fire station. Hermann means "army man". The original word was Arminius and was used as a rallying cry. Martin Luther is believed to have been the first to use the word Hermann.

1

History of Hermann

from the Rhine to the Missouri

*Hermann, which is famous for having the largest
wine cellars in the country, no municipal government,
and an entire absence of the English language, has also
an enviable reputation for its thirst.*
— St. Louis Post Dispatch
(undated older clipping)

Born in 18 B.C., Arminius was the son of a war chief in what would someday become Germany. As a youth, he was sent to Rome to learn the civilized ways, and earned his way as a military commander to receive Roman citizenship.

Upon his return to his homeland, Arminius began secretly meeting with the chieftains of other tribes. He managed to form a coalition of warriors and fought back against the oppressive Roman armies. After the successful battle of the Teutoburg Forest, Arminius drove the Roman Legions out of present-day Germany. Knowing the Roman leaders' mindset, he prepared for a counter attack and,

Photo by Dan Terry

The grave of George Bayer, who was chosen as a representative of the German Settlement Society to spearhead the settlement of the village of Hermann, which began in 1837.

after initial losses, again was able to force the Roman Army back across the Rhine River. This cost him his wife, who was captured and taken back to the capital city as a slave, and his unborn son, who would be trained as a gladiator and eventually killed for the amusement of the Roman citizens. The alliance would fall apart, and Arminius himself was later killed by his own men. But Rome would never again hold that area.

During the sixteenth century, Christian reformer Martin Luther is believed to have been the first to have used the word, "Hermann," meaning 'army man', in place of Arminius. During the Napoleonic Wars in the nineteenth century, Arminius, or "Hermann", was used as a propaganda tool, or a rallying cry.

A writer named Gottfried Duden was changing the course of a nation. Born in Germany, he traveled to the New World, and lived on a farm near present day Dutzow, Missouri. After several years, he returned to his native country where, in 1829, he penned the book "Bericht uber eine Reise nach den west lichen Staaten Nordamerika's" (Report of a journey to the western states of North America). In this book, he compared the Missouri River to their own Rhine River, and made positive remarks concerning the climate, soil and culture of the area. These writings, along with others, caused a mass migration to land bordering the lower Missouri River. Between 1830 and 1860, some 38,000 German immigrants moved to this area.

One group, called Deutsche Ansiedlungs-Gesellschaft zu Pennsylvania (German Settlement Society of Pennsylvania), was also reading Duden's work. Concerned over the erosion of German family values and the English influence on their children, their idea was to create a series of self-supporting colonies in the western United States designed with German ideals.

The area chosen for the first settlement was reported to be a paradise along the Missouri River. George Bayer, a school teacher, was assigned the duties of creating the colony. As a representative of the German Settlement Society, he purchased 11,300 acres of land for $15,600. The German-style village would be nestled in a small valley, protected on three sides by hills and bordered on the north by the Missouri River. The first of the settlers landed in the winter of 1837.

But paradise was not waiting for them. The harsh winter would take a toll on the poorly-supplied party. Their leader, Bayer, became sick before leaving Pennsylvania, sending the group alone to the wilds of Missouri. When Bayer arrived in the spring of 1838 with another group of settlers, he found his task to be overwhelming.

Bayer was given the job of general agent. He was to assign land lots to the settlers, plat out the village, provide food for the people, set up businesses, dole out justice and listen to the complaints. He was also to set up a beautiful city that the Society had mapped out for him, a city intended to rival Philadelphia. However, on their map, the land was flat and wide. In reality, the area was steep and rugged. The only part of the plan that met with success was Market Street. The founders wanted Hermann to have a street wider than Philadelphia's Market Street. Today's Market Street in Hermann is ten feet wider than its eastern counterpart.

Bayer found the tasks assigned to him to be overwhelming. Things did not go according to plan, and eventually the Society removed him from his office. Bayer was blamed for all the problems with the new town and died of a broken heart in 1839. He was buried outside the cemetery and the elders decreed that no one would be buried within 75 feet of him.

Possibly because of the fight to tame the land, or because the name was popular in the old country, the city was named "Hermann" after the warrior who had defeated the Romans 17 centuries earlier.

The soil was rocky, the area referred to as a "howling wilderness". The property many had purchased was actually bluffs or steep hills, known by locals today as "vertical acreage". Yet, the village survived—a testament to the stubborn perseverance of the German settlers.

Wild grapevines grew everywhere. The locals began planting them on the rocky hills, cultivating them the way it had been done in the old country. Soon, wineries began making spirits in the German tradition.

By the 1880's, Hermann was a regular stop for steam-driven paddle wheelers moving up the Missouri River. The train brought even more people, and the first wine festival was held in Hermann around the 1850's. Port wines, Catawba wines, sweet and dry wines were enjoyed as visitors marveled at the grapevine-covered hills that surrounded the town.

Homes were built in the German tradition of butting up close to the sidewalk. Soon, the city became a riverport town, with saloons on every corner. Stone Hill Winery became the second-largest winery in the United States and their wines won gold medals in competitions around the world. Founded in 1847, Stone Hill Winery was shipping 1,250,000 gallons of wine per year by 1900.

The White House Hotel, opened in 1869, was considered the grandest hotel between Ohio and Denver. Hermann became home to the largest general store on the Missouri River between St. Louis and Kansas City.

The town faltered in the early twentieth century. First, World War I brought a wave of anti-German sentiment that was followed by Prohibition, which forced a halt to the production of wine and beer.

Stone Hill Winery began growing mushrooms in the dark, cavernous, otherwise empty wine cellar. After Prohibition ended, the Great Depression continued to keep the wine business down. It was followed by World War II, and another wave of anti-German feelings across the country.

After Prohibition, the wineries lay dormant for nearly a half century. In 1965, Stone Hill Winery was purchased by the current owners, Jim and Betty Held. Rebuilding the winery, including what was the largest series of vaulted cellars in America, completely dug out by hand, was a daunting task. However, the rebuilding of the winery began the reformation of wine making in the Missouri River Valley. In 2008, Stone Hill produced 260,000 gallons of wine, and the area boasts other wineries such as OakGlenn, Bias, Hermannhoff, and Puchta. In addition, there are many more in nearby Berger, New Haven, and Marthasville.

Today, Hermann's old-world charm and the many festivals

Photo by Dan Terry

This plaque occupies a place of honor next to the grave of George F. Bayer, who purchased land for Hermann in 1837.

held throughout the year lure tourists from around the globe to the small hamlet on the Missouri River. From the world-famous Maifest and Octoberfest to the Old Mustang weekend and Wurstfest, there is something for everyone in Hermann. The wine drinker has a host of choices. The man who enjoys a micro-brew will find a brewery in town. And for the ghost hunter, the dead await as well.

Photo by Dan Terry

*This cannon was used to defend the village of Hermann during Price's Raid
in 1864. It was pulled from the Missouri River and given a place of honor at
the courthouse and was fired on special occasions for a number of years.*

2

Of War and Tragedy

why are riverports haunted?

As picturesque and peaceful as Hermann is today, one might believe the town was always quiet. However, any place where Man exists must have its share of conflict and Hermann is no exception.

There are the day-to-day tragedies, such as people falling victim to cancer, normal illnesses and children being orphaned due to accidents. But no town, especially an old river town like Hermann, is complete without its legendary problems—those horrible happenings that seem to echo from the past through time itself to remind us all that we, too, are mortal.

In 1838, a cholera epidemic broke out in the town. Cholera was not unheard of, especially in river towns. In 1833, the disease had invaded St. Charles just a few miles up the river from Hermann and wiped out hundreds of people there and in St. Louis. In 1848, a ship from New Orleans carrying cholera victims reintroduced the disease to the same area, again killing entire families in the St. Louis and St. Charles area. Cholera was a most-feared disease as its victims at that time had little chance of survival, but it did not offer a quick, clean death. Severe dehydration from diarrhea and nausea, causing the skin to dry out and the victims to seemingly shrink before the eyes of their loved ones. The skin became very dry and discolored, and painful stomach cramps wracked the bodies of the dying. Soon, sometimes within 18 hours, sometimes several days later, the body would simply give up life, bringing a mixture of horror, grief, and even relief to the caregivers. An epidemic of cholera brought great emotional stress, leaving scars on families and communities.

The Missouri River may seem small compared to the Mississippi, but looks can be deceiving. The calm appearance of the surface belies the eddies, underwater obstacles, strong currents and rapid floods. Any river town has, in its history, river disasters, especially a riverboat port.

Robert Fulton is remembered in history as the father of the steamboat age. However, Fulton did not invent the steamship, but instead made it a commercially-lucrative venture. Inventor John Fitch, in 1787, demonstrated the first steam-powered ship before members of the Continental Congress. He went on to create the first commercial ship, which carried passengers and cargo between Philadelphia and New Jersey. Fitch eventually had four more boats traveling the rivers and lakes, but went broke due to his lack of knowledge about boat construction, causing each one to cost more to operate than it was capable of earning. Later, Fulton made the steamship economically productive.

The early riverboats were steam driven and powered by burning wood that had to be purchased from vendors stationed along the river. Many towns sprang up around the locations where men were selling firewood to the steamers as they made their way up the river. Iron boilers, prone to explosion, pushed the mighty transports upriver. One or two tall smoke stacks belching black smoke and cinders heralded the approach of the craft for miles.

Paddlewheels on the side or rear of the vessel left a white foam in its wake as the river water churned beneath them. Most had a brow, or short bridge on the bow, which could be lowered for the transfer of passengers or cargo in ports with no docking facilities. The ships brought necessary supplies and a few luxuries, as well as people and news, to the contact-starved villages along the river.

On July 28, 1845, the steamboat *Big Hatchie* exploded just off Wharf Street. As that week's issue of the *St. Louis Weekly Reveille* reported:

"It becomes our painful duty, as faithful chroniclers of passing events, to record one of the most serious disasters that has occurred upon our waters since the explosion of the steamer Edna. The steamer Big Hatchie, Captain Frisbee, which left our port on Monday last for the Missouri River, with some 40 passengers on board, in leaving the landing at Hermann . . . on her way to St. Joseph, burst her starboard boiler with a loud explosion, which forced it straight forward, the steam discharging itself aloft, carrying away the main cabin as far as the ladies' cabin, making a perfect wreck of the boat, and spreading death and desolation among the

Photos by Dan Terry

Monument erected in memory of the 35 victims of the
"Big Hatchie" steamboat explosion that occurred in 1845.

passengers."

There are conflicting estimates of the number of victims, ranging from 35 to 50 persons dead, and many injured. But at the top of the local cemetery, placed on a steep hill overlooking the picturesque town, stands a monument dedicated to the 35 unknown or unclaimed victims of the disaster buried in a mass grave there. Some bodies were lost to the swirling waters of the Missouri River. The dead and dying were brought to shore and placed in homes and businesses along Wharf Street. While not the only maritime disaster in Hermann's history, it was the worst.

In 1870, the Steamer *Washington*, being used as a ferry at Hermann, burned to the waterline, killing at least one person. Firewood, stored next to the boiler itself, caught on fire, setting the bow of the sturdy little ship on fire as well. Captain Heckmann attempted to steer the vessel to shore, but the fire destroyed the steering apparatus as it consumed the boat. A man on the bank, identified as Henry Maushund, rowed out to the burning ship and rescued most of its passengers and crew. One woman jumped into the river to escape the flames and drowned when her water-logged clothing pulled her under the surface.

According to Dorothy Heckmann Shrader, in her book *Steamboat Legacy: The Life and Times of a Steamboat Family,* in 1880, several children in the city died of typhoid fever, diphtheria, and rheumatism. Her own brothers and sisters fell ill, but survived. A neighbor lost two children and the city lost several more of its youth.

The only known lynching in Hermann occurred in June 1883. Two young men stopped at the farm home of William Collier near the community of Bem, several miles from Hermann, and asked for breakfast. As Mrs. Collier was preparing the meal, she overheard them making plans to rob the W. P. Burchard store in Hermann. After they left, she told her husband of their plans, and he rode hard for Hermann to inform Burchard of the plan.

Immediately, Burchard, his young son, William, and the farmer, William Collier, armed themselves and went to set a trap for the thieves. However, they were too late. Upon their arrival, the two robbers were already inside the store, speaking with a clerk. When challenged by the store owner, a gunfight began and young William

Burchard was killed. The two robbers, turned murderers, fled out of the back of the building, one of them falling dead a few yards outside. The other managed to escape.

A crowd turned out for the funeral of William Burchard, the boy who had been killed while defending his father's store. The unlucky thief's body was never identified, but he was buried in an unmarked grave near the present Highway 19 bridge at Dry Fork Creek.

Some 55 years later, following a flood, his skeleton was exposed in its lonely tomb. His bones were moved 20 feet away and reburied, still alone.

The second suspect apparently made his way to Rosebud where he sought medical attention for his injuries. A few days later, a Hermann doctor heard about a gunshot victim in Rosebud, some 25 miles away. He went to check, and discovered it was the second robber, who was being cared for by good people who were unaware of how he had been injured. The doctor personally took the man into custody and delivered him to nearby Owensville, where a cell was hastily constructed.

A few nights later, a mob gathered to lynch him. He extinguished the only light in the room and hid behind the door. When the door was forced open and the mob entered, he joined the group of vigilantes calling for the death of the suspect, and slowly made his way out. Once free, he stole a horse and headed for nearby New Haven where a ferry would spirit him across the river to freedom.

Due to the wet, muddy conditions, it was not hard to track him. He didn't make it to the ferry and was captured again at Detmold. This time, he was taken to the county seat and locked up in the calaboose in Hermann. On June 4, 1883, a group of men went to the jail, knocked out the deputy, and took the alleged killer into their custody. About 150 yards outside the city limits, they threw a rope over a large sycamore tree, placed a noose around the neck of the suspect and asked if he had any last words. The man had originally claimed to be Whitney, but finally identified himself as J.W. Fisher from Chatam Hills, Virginia. He said he was sure he did not kill the boy, and begged for forgiveness.

His penance for the crime came at the end of the rope. After

Photo by Dan Terry

Today, the Civil War cannon that was put to good use in 1864 stands guard at the Gasconade County Courthouse.

he died, his body was left there until morning, when the sheriff and deputy took charge of the inquest. It ended with "He's dead." The investigation went no further.

Great floods, drownings, hotel fires, even a courthouse fire added to the list of disasters inflicted on the German community. But one of the proudest moments came during the Civil War, and it was far from disaster.

Many Hermann men had already joined the militias and were away fighting when General Sterling Price, a former Missouri governor, was leading one last desperate charge into Missouri in an attempt to capture St. Louis and the capital, Jefferson City, for the Confederacy. Coming up from Arkansas, he fought a harder-than-expected battle near Arcadia, known as the Battle of Pilot Knob.

Price headed for Jefferson City. His men burned the depot at Washington, then stopped a train in Miller's Landing, which is present-day New Haven, and took over 200 Sharps rifles and clothing. Moving on into Hermann, they burned the train and destroyed the tracks.

Just as the Confederates rounded a bluff entering Hermann,

they were met with a barrage of cannon fire. The unit retreated and tried another approach, but were again driven back by artillery fire.

This went on for hours. The Confederates moved cautiously, afraid ground troops might be backing the artillery. Little did they know that the city had been waiting for them. With their one small cannon, the men of the town hid the women and children in nearby caves and on Graf's Island on the Missouri River. Despite the weakness of their small force, they devised a strategy to defend the town and to put forth a show of strength. They fired the cannon, then quickly moved it and fired again. When it appeared that the enemy was about to make an assault on their location, the townsmen dropped the cannon into the river and beat a hasty retreat.

While the "battle" itself was insignificant, it allowed the extra time needed for General McNeil to bring in his regiment, further fortifying Jefferson City. It helped stop General Price from taking Missouri for the South.

When the story came to light, the little cannon was pulled from the river and placed near the courthouse overlooking the Missouri River, where it was fired off on special occasions such as the Fourth of July. One year, they packed too large a powder charge for the abused, aging cannon, splitting its sides. Today, the hero of the Battle of Hermann sits on a stone brace in front of the courthouse, overlooking the community it fought for nearly 150 years ago.

The history of Hermann has had the same highs and lows as any other community and, like other river communities, the spirits of the past linger along the streets and buildings, waiting to be remembered.

Photo by Dan Terry

Wine Valley Inn is a great place to stay as can be attested to by present clientele and past guests, who just don't want to leave.

3

Wine Valley Inn
some folks just can't leave work

The imposing brick structure is located at the corner of Fourth and Market streets. The flat roof is guarded by four towers, one on each corner. Designs in the tile work between the towers break up the green sides on the top floor, giving it an eye-pleasing appearance from every angle.

The building was constructed in 1899 by August Begemann, who built it for his son, Louis. For years, it was known as the Louis Begemann store. August Begemann had emigrated to Hermann in 1855, and he eventually became the wealthiest merchant in town. He built, or purchased, buildings on almost every street in town, including Wharf Street.

The mercantile business was on the street level. The family lived on the second floor, and the third floor was mostly empty.

It was a large general store for many years. In its various incarnations, it has since been a real estate office, an insurance office, low-income housing and even a palm reader's parlor. The owner bought a second building, built in 1905, just down Fourth Street from the Begemann property and both structures were utilized as low-income housing. In 2003, they were purchased by Begemann Bldg., LLC, who undertook their renovation. Today, they house a bed and breakfast and small shop.

Jeanie Schultz has lived in Hermann for a long time. When she took a management job at the bed and breakfast, the idea of resident ghosts never crossed her mind.

That changed when a salesman came in. As he went through his sales pitch, he kept looking toward the conference room, finally asking Jeanie if the building was haunted. The salesman claimed he had a knack for photographing ghosts, and asked for permission to attempt to do so. After photographing the lobby, he showed her some pictures depicting large, glowing orbs. A guest came down from the second floor one day and said he believed the place was haunted.

One day, the manager discovered the swinging door to the garbage can storage area was swinging as if someone had just put trash in it. But, she was the only one with access to it that day. Jeanie watched as the small hatch swung back and forth, never stopping.

However, one of the most convincing occurrences took place when the ghost got "handsy".

"I was bent over the dryer, putting in sheets. I felt a pinch on my butt, like a goose. I thought my husband had come in and I turned to yell at him, then realized I was alone in the building."

Jeanie told the spirit that if he wanted to stay, he could help with the laundry. So far, the ghost has refused to assist.

Another employee reported hearing two men talking upstairs in the second building. Believing someone had stayed the night there, the worker returned to Jeanie, who assured him that none of the guests were staying over from the night before. Jeanie and others have also reported hearing these two men speak in loud voices, but had never been able to understand the words.

The last straw came one night after Jeanie had locked up as usual and left the building. In the morning, she discovered that a bottle of wine that she was certain she had left in the refrigerator the night before, had been moved from the fridge through the kitchen and the dining area and left on a table inside the conference room. No guests or employees confessed to moving the wine. Jeanie was sure something supernatural was going on.

After a casual discussion, the Spookstalker was called to investigate. Jeanie agreed to our coming in for an investigation after meeting us there. She took Sherri and me for a walk around the building and we spoke with some of the other employees.

This 1911 postcard depicts the old Begemann-Armin Store/ Restaurant in Haunted Hermann. This building is now Wine Valley Inn.

One young maid told that she had seen, out of the corner of her eye, people walking into the room behind her. When she turned around, no one was there. She was alone—at least she was the only living person in the room.

Both Jeanie and her co-manager, Sonya Birk, are certain the basement of the second building is haunted. Both report "creepy feelings" there, and their husbands both hate going down there alone. One of the men said he always feels as if someone is watching when he is working on the furnace.

On June 14, Sherri and I went in to investigate. We brought in our usual team of sensitives, including Tim Clifton, Theresa Reavey, and Steven LaChance. A local ghost investigator, Ted Prusinowski, who owns a haunted house on Wharf Street, also assisted.

I informed the team of the hot spots, being careful not to give them too much information. Steven's attention was diverted to the conference room, and he asked if he could go in there. We had not told him about the salesman.

Tim and Steven went into the room. Soon, they called for Theresa to join them. At that time, I went in and my attention was directed to a corner of the room, near the ceiling. All three psychics agreed there was a spirit hovering there. I took some photos, and in each one a single orb showed up in that corner.

Tim began telling me of the feelings he was getting from the

23

spirit. He was presenting himself as a 42-year-old man, wearing a business suit with suspenders. An approximate time of his life was uncertain, but Tim and Steven both believed he limped. Tim said it was caused by an illness, and suggested polio.

I hooked up the Ovilus. The first word to come out was "safe."

Tim asked if the spirit felt safe there. The second word was "property".

Suddenly, Tim got an idea. Expressing reluctance, he said he felt as though the spirit had been stabbed with a fork by a loved one. I thought that was a wild idea, but Steven agreed that the spirit had been stabbed by a loved one. Tim again said the image of a fork kept coming into his mind.

The Ovilus said, "property", "stair", "step". Tim pushed the word "safe", asking again if the spirit felt safe there. The word "safe" suddenly issued again from the speakers. The spirit was trying to tell us something.

The spirit, according to Tim, did not like Theresa being in the room. She left, taking the rest of the investigators and managers to the basement. There, a cigar bar is currently being built. A walk-in humidor, awaiting installation of a door, is situated near a stone wall that has wine casks built into it. Concrete steps had just been poured leading to the street level. In this room, Theresa believes there is a residual spirit of a woman. Residual ghosts have no intelligence but are more like an imprint onto the scene.

Upstairs, Tim and Steven continued to speak with the spirit. The word "deed" had come from the speakers, along with "safe". We decided to stop at that point and try again later.

The group met up again in the dining room. As we spoke with the managers, Sonya said her husband's father had been a real estate agent, and his office had been in that room. Sonya had not been a part of the investigation in there, and was not aware of what had transpired. In fact, other than her husband's fear of the basement of the second building and her own visions of fleeting shadows in her peripheral vision, Sonya claimed to have no belief in ghosts.

This was about to change. I asked if her father-in-law limped, and she said he did, due to pain in his feet caused by diabetes.

Photo by Sherri Terry

This orb was photographed in a storeroom at Wine Valley Inn, indicating the presence of a ghost there.

Remembering Jeanie's account of being pinched, I asked if he considered himself a ladies' man, and would do something like that. Smiling, Sonya said she "wouldn't put it past him".

Suddenly, Steven turned to face the door to the conference room. He said "It's out here, watching us." Sherri took the photo over his shoulder, which showed an orb just outside the door to that room.

We decided to check out the basement to the second building. Along the way, Jeanie's husband, Phil, made the comment as we passed a storage area off the kitchen, that he often felt uncomfortable there, almost as if he were being watched. Sherri took a single photo of the area as we passed by. A large, very bright orb was captured against the wall in that photo, where Phil felt there was activity.

Due to the presence of guests, we were unable to investigate the area where men had been heard arguing. In the basement, a high EMF near the furnace may explain the feeling the men had experienced, that of being watched while working there. High electro-magnetic fields have been known to cause feelings of paranoia and even nausea.

But the sensitives also believed something else was there. Following them, the KII meter began to flash, indicating the presence of unexplained electromagnetic energy. The flashing was intermitten, coming and going, unlike an electrical source of the readings that would have remained constant as long as the power was on.

Following them into another room, we were told drug users and, possibly meth cooks, had lived there when the building was used for low-income housing. But the psychics were feeling something else; the presence of a spirit—that of an older man, who felt that this was his home and we were invaders. I turned on the Ovilus. Behind me, Sherri and Ted were using the KII meters, which began to spike. Tim and Steven sensed a person standing near the location of an old bathroom. Taking the Ovilus there, it said the word "Leave" and shut itself off. I have never seen the device turn itself off before. I checked the batteries, which were new and solidly connected.

Suddenly, Sonya came into the basement. I went in to speak with her, and her news was so intriguing that I called the other investigators in.

Sonya had contacted her husband. The conference room is where her father-in-law's office had been. And in the corner of the room, where Tim and Steven had felt a spirit hovering, had been a drop ceiling. When they removed the ceiling, they found that *the combination to his safe had been stored there!*

This may explain the word "safe", and the spirit remaining there. But the confirmation was not over. Sonya reported that when she told her husband what had been said, he confirmed that his father was once *stabbed with a fork by his brother!* Both psychics felt that he had been stabbed by a loved one, and Tim was certain it was with a fork. This night, I began to change my opinion of the psychics, giving them more credence than before.

We checked another room where another hermit spirit apparently just wanted to be left alone. When the door was opened, several believed they saw a mist in the room, and it moved through a wall. While inside, attempting to make contact, Sherri felt as though the spirit was around her. Tim confirmed the ghost was standing behind her, as did the fact that the hair on both of her arms was standing straight up. In all of our years of investigating, I had never seen this. Tim said the ghost was attempting to intimidate Sherri, since she was the only woman in the room at that time. He picked the wrong woman to attempt to scare.

The next day, when I spoke with Jeanie, she told me that her young daughter, who had asked why they were unlocking that door, had asked if she could go in there. Stepping inside, the middle-school-aged girl said her hair had been touched and she saw a mist dart away. This confirmed what our team would experience several hours later.

Since this room was used only for storage, we left the spirit to his solitude and returned to the conference room. Ted had gone in alone and reported his KII meter spiked to red. We all went into the room and I set up the Ovilus.

The speakers began issuing several words: "stair", "safe", "step", "art". Suddenly, the word "realtor" emerged. Sonya was asked to come up with a question that only she and her father-in-law would know the answer to.

She asked the spirit, "Who used a micrometer for a hammer?" The Ovilus remained silent. She again asked who had used this measuring device as a hammer. The speakers answered: "sister", "Maupin".

Sonya laughed with surprise. She informed the group that it was his sister, who had owned a business off Maupin Street in New Haven with her husband, who had used the micrometer to pound something. What shocked me is that the word "Maupin" is NOT in the dictionary of the Ovilus. Technically, the word should not have come out of it.

A short time later, the Ovilus speakers said "George". When asked if that name meant anything, Sonya confirmed that George was the name of her late father-in-law's business partner, who also shared this office. Sonya, who had been a self-described skeptic, left that night a little more open to the paranormal.

But the biggest surprise of the night was not from the Ovilus, or an EVP. While speaking with the spirit, it was mentioned by Sonya that the wife of the spirit was still alive. When I asked if the spirit was waiting for her to pass, an audible "No" was heard from the other side of the conference room. Tim began to say something, but I stopped him, asking "did anyone say no?" Everyone in the room had heard the word spoken, but no one admitted to saying it. Additionally, no one was on that side of the room at the time.

We stopped the investigation around midnight, content that we could say the building is haunted. The spirit there is content to be where he is comfortable—and seems to enjoy his wine—a true citizen of Hermann.

Whenever I take up a newspaper, I seem to see Ghosts gliding between the lines. There must be Ghosts all the country over, as thick as the sand of the sea. . . . We are, one and all, so pitifully afraid of the light.

—Henrik Ibsen, *Ghosts*

Photos by Dan Terry

Buy the Book Book Store is a great place to find books of every genre, but don't be surprised if you encounter a vanishing canine.

4

Buy the Book

you don't have to believe to see them

Through years of investigations, I've met a lot of skeptics. Some really don't believe. Others just like to argue. One young lady had some incredible things going on, including objects appearing in her apartment, lights and showers coming on when no one was home, and sounds of invisible people talking, but she swore she didn't believe, because if she did, she would not have been able to go home at night.

But the really interesting folks are the ones who start the conversation with, "I don't believe in ghosts, but here is what happened to me . . . " I get some of my best stories from these self-proclaimed skeptics, who don't believe in ghosts but have seen or heard so much.

That happened at Buy the Book, a used bookstore, art and photo gallery, located at 303 Schiller Street in Hermann. The symbol on the sign outside shows what appears to be a yin and yang symbol, using a dragon and phoenix inside. When *Missouri Shadows* came out, I did a book signing there. The owner told me a story and I went back to talk to her again when I was preparing to write this book.

When you walk into the store, stacks and rows of books and

art fill the room. A counter sits just inside the door and behind that is a lovely, grandmotherly lady with a story. But she doesn't believe in ghosts.

Pat Wendleton started the store four years ago with her son. He has since moved on but she remains to run the store alone, enjoying time with her patrons who often come in just for a quiet respite from the day-to-day grind of the outside world.

Pat remembered me and welcomed me warmly. When I told her why I was there, she was more than happy to help. That is just Pat's personality—always eager to help and make a new friend. But before starting her story, she had to prologue it.

"I don't believe in ghosts, you know."

"But . . ."

Pat began her story. "I was sitting in the next room, in that chair right there." She pointed just inside the door to another room, where a large, overstuffed chair occupied a space amidst tall bookshelves. "A dog, a lab, just appeared on the floor, walking toward my side of the room. It wasn't corporeal, but I knew it was a black lab. It didn't look at me—just walked into the wall next to where I was sitting. It wasn't frightening at all. I was never afraid."

But she doesn't believe.

This wasn't the only time Pat has seen the canine ghost. The next time, it was a shadow, walking across the floor just as it had before. The shadow was not against the wall, just there in the floor. Again, Pat knew she was looking at a black lab, and yet knew the dog wasn't really there. And again, it disappeared into the wall.

Pat spoke about this to her son, who said that while he had never seen the ghost, he always felt "something" in that room. Pat also told a friend, who told her the building had been owned by an optometrist. The old man, affectionately called "Doc", liked animals and had allowed his patients to bring their pets into the waiting room rather than leave them outside in the humid Missouri heat. Her friend described a large, old black lab that would come there and visit with the humans and other animals, then leave. Pat quickly informed her friend that she didn't believe in ghosts. "Honey," the friend said, "I couldn't care less if you believe it or not."

The building has been an attorney's office, Doc's office, and a massage therapy center before Pat opened the bookstore. The room does have a comfortable feeling to it. Imagine sitting in your favorite, overstuffed lounge chair, books around you, roaring fire protecting you from the howling winter outside, and your favorite dog at your feet as you sit quietly contemplating life.

Same kind of place, except the dog at your feet is a ghost.

Photos by Dan Terry

Lyndee's Restaurant is a favorite among troopers, past and present.

5

Lyndee's Restaurant
the safest restaurant in town

On the south end of Market Street, leading out of town, sits Lyndee's Restaurant. Lynn Helming owns the home-style eatery, and her daughter, Kecia, now manages it for her mom. Lynn has owned the restaurant for 13 years. And for at least 13 years, it's been haunted.

I found out about the haunting in a strange way. A local in New Haven, familiar with my interest in ghosts, knew Kecia and had worked part time at the restaurant. He knew of the legends and had told Kecia he knew me. Kecia and Lynn are interested in the paranormal and were eager for me to come in.

The building was originally a garage and gas station built by Ralph Grannemann. In those early days, there was very little between the towns of Owensville, Rosebud and Hermann other than long, curvy, dark roads. Wrecks were pulled into the garage from all over the county. Later, the business was known as George's Service Station. Lynn recalled that the owner, identified only as George, had died in the building, where he had spent a lot of happy hours.

Harold Hildebrand bought the business later after Ralph added a restaurant. Because it was often the only place open at night in the entire county, all the state troopers, deputies, and local police frequented the establishment, giving it the nickname "Trooper Heaven"—a name by which it became well known.

Harold was a former police officer and allegedly ruled his employees with an iron fist. Things were done his way or you could look for another job. A deputy named Harry Heberle used to hang out in Trooper Heaven, and he and Harold were as much a part of the decor as the old photos on the wall.

In May of 2008, Sherri and I, along with friends, Tim Clifton, his daughter, Ginny, and Steven LaChance, went to Lyndee's. Tim and Steven had recently been involved in quite a few demonic cases, and I thought they could use a Casper hunt. Kecia and Lynn were waiting inside for us.

We were greeted warmly and the two had many questions about Steven's time in the Union Screaming House. Soon, we began discussing the haunted history of Lyndee's restaurant. One interesting fact was that on a night over a year before, a burglar had broken into several different stores, stealing money and valuables.

One of the stores was Lyndee's. It was around 11:30 P.M. when he broke a small window with a flashlight, reached in and opened the deadbolt. Inside, the money from that day had been left on the bar in a green, plastic-zippered bank bag with the name of the bank emblazoned on the side. Next to it, a waitress had carelessly left her tip money, several bills and some change, lying out in the open. None of the places that were hit that night could have been an easier mark.

But, for some reason, the burglar was scared off. It was the only business he did not get any money from that night. What might have frightened him away from the scene?

For 12 years, Lynn had ignored the creepy feelings of being watched. She and Kecia, along with several of their employees, had heard their names called from an empty room. One waitress remembered seeing a man in a white shirt through the service window walking around the kitchen. She ran in to see who was in the kitchen, Once inside, there was no visible human present. According to Lynn, some of their regular customers have seen the same man walking around in the kitchen, only to disappear when one of the employees was told about it.

One day, several customers watched as a framed photograph, which had been hanging in the same location for years, suddenly fell. Well, not so much fell as became unattached from the wall, and glided away from the wall as if it had wings. It swooped in an arc, landing gently like a glider and sliding under a table. There was no fan and there were no wind currents, certainly nothing like the amount of wind necessary to send a heavy-framed photo flying across the hall and landing under a table, without striking anything. Employees replaced the photo, which was not damaged in any way and they even tried to make it fall again, to no avail.

One employee, while working a fairly busy supper crowd, saw a chubby, curly-haired, freckle-faced boy of about ten standing in the aisle. Thinking he was looking for the restroom, she stopped and asked the boy if he needed help. The cherub-faced child looked up and said nothing, but made eye contact with the waitress. Believing he was shy, she asked again if he needed something. Slowly, the child faded out of sight.

Confused, the waitress asked if anyone had seen the child she was talking to. A customer told her he watched as she spoke to the air, but did not see a child in front of her as she leaned down. No one else had seen the child, who had stood before her only a second before. The waitress quit on the spot, leaving the restaurant and never returning.

Neither Kecia nor Lynn have felt any malevolence or fear themselves, apart from the idea that they were alone in a haunted building. But Kecia did mention an interesting occurrence that had taken place a few weeks earlier.

She had been out on a Saturday night with a group of friends, returning to the restaurant for a nightcap after the bar had closed. She was standing behind the bar with her friends, including a man she had just met, when a glass mysteriously lifted itself from the shelf under the bar and slowly moved around the side to the area between bars where, in full view of the group, it fell to the floor, shattering loudly. The party was over; everyone left hurriedly. Interestingly, the man she had just met that night was arrested the following week for severely beating his girlfriend in a nearby town.

Are the restaurant and its owner being protected by some otherworldly guardian? That's what we were called in to find out.

As we were discussing the past, Tim Clifton was doing an assessment of the building and its invisible inhabitants. At least, they are invisible to most of us. Tim walked back in and stated he had seen a male spirit in the back dining room. He described the ghost as tall and thin, with a mustache and wearing a white shirt. He had not been present when we were told about the man in the white shirt being seen in the kitchen. After hearing the description, Lynn said it sounded exactly like Harold Hildebrand.

Cameras were set up in that rear dining room. As Steven and Tim attempted to make contact, Ginny and I both saw dark-colored orbs shooting across the ceiling above our heads. Sprites, or small flashes of light, indicating the presence of spirits, erupted in the corner of the room. I walked over to the area, and Tim said I had angered the spirit by standing in its place.

Well, I've angered a few before. I remained as Tim and Steven spoke of what they believed they had found. Both agreed it was a male entity, possibly middle aged. Because of the history of Hermann, Tim attempted to speak to the ghostly visitor in German.

Suddenly, Steven began laughing loudly. The very atmosphere in the room seemed to lighten, as if the walls themselves were humored by the words. Steven relayed that the ghost was laughing at Tim over his attempts to speak in German, that he was proud of being an American. It was as if the spirit wanted to know, "What country are you in?"

Tim then made contact with what he believed to be a child. Steven and Ginny both agreed. With the KII meter in hand, Tim and I approached the corner where they thought the child was. Steven said the spirit was intimidated by the two large men walking toward him and began cringing. We both backed away from the corner.

Steven sensed the child had been killed in an accident and his spirit had remained in the vehicle as it was towed to the garage. He had remained in the building, afraid to move on. Kecia mentioned the child-sized table with checker and tic-tac-toe games that were set up in the main part of the dining area. After the clean-up crew tidied up and left them neatly on the table, they would often be found strewn around haphazardly. Ginny said the spirit liked to play with the toys left there.

During this time, I could see what appeared to be movement through the crack in the sliding door between the two dining areas. I stepped inside that room and observed a shadow person walk quickly into the kitchen. I checked the area, finding no one. While in there, I heard a heavy bang as if a glass salt shaker was being slammed down on the table. I ran back into that room, again finding nothing out of place.

I started back to the rear dining room. To the left of the sliding door, a pair of western saloon-type doors separated the restrooms from the dining area. Inside those doors, I heard what sounded like fingernails scratching the wall. Again, I found nothing to explain this. But at that moment, Steven had asked the spirit to make a noise for them.

Tim suddenly made contact with another spirit. This one, which Tim seemed to channel, was acting out his death. Tim felt fluid in his lungs. Lynn suggested one of the former owners had died of congestive heart failure.

Then, Tim described extreme pain, and an inability to breathe—a pain in the chest—and, out of nowhere, hot rain. Tim began to get too caught up with empathy for the spirit. Steven had to force him to break the connection.

A discussion later led us to a logical explanation for what Tim had experienced. A mass grave for the victims of the explosion and sinking of the *Big Hatchie* steamboat was in the city cemetery only a few hundred yards away. On the "other side", a sensitive such as Tim might shine like a lighthouse in the darkness to wandering spirits. The pain, drowning, and hot rain of an exploding boiler could possibly be the last living memories of a victim of that tragedy.

We took a break as the women attempted to make contact with the spirit of the child. Then everyone relaxed a few minutes and returned for another try.

We all sat down around the room and the lights were turned out. The small, green light on the back of my video camera was reflecting on the glass doors of a china hutch in the corner, casting an eerie glow on that side of the room. I noticed a break in the light as if it were blinking. I knew it wasn't due to a low battery because it was plugged into the wall. Again, the stream of light was broken intermittently as if something was crossing between the small light on the camera and the glass panes of the hutch. We were not alone.

While running the EVP session, Steven suddenly stopped speaking and wanted to say something, but seemed reluctant to do so. He kept saying it was silly, or we would not believe it. Finally, he came to the point:

"Law Enforcement. I am seeing cops. Police." Ginny agreed. "I knew you were going to say that," she said. Lynn reminded us that Harold was a former police officer. Steven replied that this was someone else.

The activity became stronger. Strangely, Steven asked what cologne Tim or I might be wearing. We both replied none. He said he was smelling the odor of Old Spice aftershave. Tim agreed that he was also sensing an odor that wasn't there before, but could not identify it.

The odor seemed to blanket my face, as if it had been blown into my nose. But I identified it immediately. I told the others that what they were smelling was cherry-flavored pipe tobacco, as my father had smoked the same type.

Tim concurred. Then, the odor dissipated around me, and Kecia detected it. Next, it moved again from Kecia to Tim and Steven, who nearly gagged on the strength of the smell. It moved back to me, then back to Kecia, as if walking a line between the four of us. Steven said he was getting a name . . . "Harry". The unexplained odor continued to move from person to person. He wanted his message out.

I suggested a former deputy of the county that I had known before his untimely death in a tractor accident. Steven disagreed. Then, Lynn reminded us of Harry Heberle, a former deputy who used to hang out there with Harold. That's when she told us about the nickname of the place, Trooper Heaven.

Suddenly, the room seemed to explode in a flurry of supernatural activity. The green light began to flash again, the odor of pipe tobacco continued to flit between us, and everyone in the room broke out in laughter. The spirits were happy! They had been identified.

We stopped for the night. Lynn told us the story of a psychic who had told her there were ghosts in her store, but they were "like her night watchmen, guarding the place." This explained the thief leaving quickly, without touching the money that had been left on the counter. Steven mentioned the unlikely way I had learned about the haunting. He believed there was a connection, a brotherhood of cops, that caused me to be here to assist them one last time.

The restaurant is still open today, advertising the area's best frog legs on Friday nights. Usually, once a month, a psychic comes in from Iowa to do readings.

Jacqui Carpenter has been a practicing spiritual medium for over 35 years. In 2007, she and her daughter Beth, a psychic in her own right, formed the International Paranormal Research Association, Inc., which uses standard guidelines and protocol in gathering evidence. Jacqui also hosts her own internet radio show and an internet TV show called "Seekers of the Paranormal", with episodes available at her web site. Jacqui and her talents were instrumental in uncovering the truth behind the Jefferson County, Missouri, haunting called "The Morse Mill Project."

The first time Jacqui walked into the restaurant, she sensed a man in the back room. When asked about him, Lynn just laughed, because so many people had seen the same man. One of her helpers was using the restroom when the doorknob began to rattle and turn. When he attempted to leave, he discovered the door had been locked from the outside. Then, suddenly, the light went out.

Other practical jokes played by the spirits included a handle flying off the sliding door and hitting Jacqui in front of witnesses, and water turning on in the restrooms. Jacqui says that each time she is there, she sees three spirits, including an older man, a woman, and a child. "The boy is my favorite," Jacqui said. "I'm sure he is the practical joker."

No trip to Hermann is complete without a stop at Lyndee's. Come in for the frog legs; stay for the spirits. They're waiting for you.

Photos by Dan Terry

The picturesque Hermann Riverfront harbors gruesome secrets from the past.

6

Wharf Street

a place of mystery and spirits

In its heyday, Wharf Street was as active as any seaport of an equal-sized town on the seashore. By 1900, Hermann was shipping over 1.25 million gallons of wine per year from Stone Hill Winery alone. The largest general store between St. Louis and Kansas City competed with three other mercantile stores to sell to the locals as well as to immigrants and others who were part of the westward migration.

Many of the disasters along Wharf Street have already been discussed. The explosion of the *Big Hatchie* steamboat killed possibly as many as 50 people, with at least 35 unnamed victims brought to Wharf Street, and then buried in a mass grave across town. The ferry boat, *Washington*, burned to the water line, with at least one and possibly two deaths.

Wharf Street saw both great joy and great tragedy. The Boston Philharmonic Ladies Band played at the White House Hotel, which was once considered to be one of the grandest hotels from Ohio to Denver. In 1886, a fire destroyed Monnig's store as well as Ettmuller's office and the White House Hotel. The fire had been started by Gussie Pfautsch, who was burned badly. It took three months to rebuild the hotel, and the main balcony was not rebuilt until 2009, 123 years later.

Around 1875, a local named Dan Skinner was standing on the bow of the steamer *Light Western* against the advice of the captain. Skinner lost his balance, and fell overboard. Captain Wohlt stopped the engine, but the vessel still went over Skinner, who came up in the wake of the ship. He appeared to be attempting to swim. A life ring was thrown near him; however, Skinner did not try to grab it. When the boat got close, Skinner went under and disappeared.

The body was found a month later lodged in the limb of a tree that leaned down into the water many miles downstream. A local doctor managed to make an identification before the body slipped from his grasp and returned to the water, never to be seen again.

Another drowning took place in January 1887. John Land and William Monnig had crossed the frozen river to attend a sale. A sudden rain caused warmer water to flow down to the river, weakening the ice covering. Land convinced Monnig to attempt a crossing, even though they had already broken through the ice near the shore. Fifty yards from the shore, the ice broke completely through, and Land slid beneath the white surface into the cold water beneath. Monnig also broke through, but after a struggle succeeded in making it to shore, where he was found, taken to a local store, and placed in a warm bed. Land's body was later discovered and buried.

Johann Worley, age 24, drowned one Sunday in June while bathing in the river. His clothes were found on the bank, but the body was never recovered.

In February 1905, Hattie Parrot was coming off the steamer *Lora*, at 8:30 P.M. when she slipped and fell into the ice-cold water below. An anxious and heartbroken city was on edge for the next 57 hours, when her body was finally located.

The same month, the county courthouse, situated on the bluffs above the river, went up in flames giving off a glow that could be seen for miles.

This, along with the cholera epidemics and the normal, rough life along the river, may have contributed to the area

Photo by Ted Prusinowski
*Photo of ghost found in drop ceiling
at 206 Wharf Street.*

becoming a center of paranormal activity.

Ted and Debbie Prusinowski were looking for a place to call their own after retirement. They looked at the building located at 206 Wharf Street, less than 100 feet from the railroad, and saw a wonderful home awaiting them, but a lot of work would have to be done to make it into a home. Ted even wondered if trains ever ran by their home. Little did he know that between the coal, freight and Amtrack trains, over 65 trains would pass his house daily.

Built on speculation by Rudolph Schlender in 1861, the building was sold to Ferdinand Metzler in 1862. Metzler turned the three-story building into a hotel, running it until 1865, when he sold it to Gotfried Ackerman. It was sold again in 1867 to Ernst Lessel, who closed the hotel and rented the building to Charles Sandberger, who stored wine there for shipment up and down the river.

The building switched owners several more times, becoming a Masonic Hall in 1892. Freemasonry is a fraternal organization that, legend says, arose from the stone masons who constructed King Solomon's temple. Legend also claims that their ranks were swelled by rogue knights on the run after the Knights Templar were destroyed by a French king and the Pope because of Satanic practices.

While the organization is extremely charitable, it is also steeped in ritual and secrecy. Rumors fly that the Masons practice some arcane form of religion from ancient Egypt, or that the Masonic Lodge is working to bring about the New World Order. Many conspiracy theorists believe that the Masonic Lodge brought about the founding of the United States, and that the back of an American dollar bill is loaded with secret Masonic symbols.

I first met Ted and Debbie Prusinowski at a book signing at Lyndee's Restaurant in Hermann. They were both eager to share photos and stories of ghosts. Debbie is sensitive and probably empathetic. Ted couldn't wait to learn how to ghost hunt and wanted me to teach him. Ted even offered to carry the equipment just to get the opportunity to train as a ghost hunter.

Oh, and did he mention he lives in a haunted place?

After Ted and Debbie worked with us on the John Busch Brewery in Washington and Wine Valley Inn investigations, Sherri and I went to Ted's house. We entered at the ground floor level and were transported by elevator to the living section on the second floor, then again up to the third floor bedroom. Space in the residence was filled with articles ranging from portraits of Catholic saints to a full-size replica of a Polish knight's armor, complete with leopard skin cape and feathered headdress. It was almost like a Scooby-Doo episode, ghost hunting in a eerie museum.

But first, Ted showed us a photograph he had taken when he was trying to determine the amount of work that would be necessary to fix the ceiling of the first floor. He popped through the drop ceiling and took the photo, then put it on the computer. There, in the corner, was a misty, white face of what appeared to be a man with a Vandyke-style beard and a bandage on his head.

Debbie is sensitive to the otherworld. On a visit to Poland, she could see knights waiting for battle in a field near a castle. She refused to go to the Auschwitz concentration camp while visiting there because of the residual feelings of the million Jews killed there, along with gypsies, Poles, and others Hitler deemed "Undesirable."

She's heard a disembodied woman's voice speaking to Ted, which he did not hear. She feels the presence of the lost souls on each floor. They've heard the sounds of a party upstairs, where the Masons used to have their meetings. They've heard knockings, and have gotten EVPs of a spirit voice calling the name of her niece.

Believing the face in the photo was a soldier, as General Price's Missouri invasion marched through Hermann, I attempted to make contact with the spirit. However, the Ovilus seemed to insist we go upstairs. It continually repeated the words "up" . . . "step" .

. . "upstairs" . . . After a 30-minute attempt to make contact, Ted, Sherri and I took the elevator up.

The Ovilus was strangely quiet during the ascent. As we moved up in the old electric elevator, it should have detected changes in temperature and humidity. The EMF had been chatting away. The doors opened on the third floor, and as I stepped out, the Ovilus said "Angel." At first, I thought it was finally testing the atmosphere. But as I stepped out, as cops do, I looked around and up. There, on the top of the elevator, was a silver casting of a winged angel.

Once Debbie joined us, we began again. Through the course of the investigation, the speakers connected to the Ovilus overheated and shut down twice. This had never happened before. The speakers shot out two words together, "ferry boat". I asked if the spirit had been aboard the steamer, *Washington*. The very next word out of the Ovilus was "Correct."

I asked for a name. The Ovilus immediately said, "Paul". I replied "Okay, Paul, . . ." and before I could ask another question, the word "Peter" came out. I said "Ok, is it Paul or Peter?" For the first time since purchasing the Ovilus, the word "Jesus" issued forth. Later, when we turned the lights on, Debbie asked if it could be talking about the silver casting above the Ovilus. There, hanging on the wall, were several arches, each with a different saint framed within the arch. Could they be Peter, Paul and Jesus?

Debbie decided to go downstairs. As she left, I was speaking about the ferry when the KII meter spiked for the first time that night. We thought it might have been caused by the elevator, but when Debbie returned, it did not go off. Sherri asked what I had been talking about when it went off, and I replied, "Were you on the *Washington* when it burned?" The KII spiked to red again for the second and final time that night.

Both Ted and Debbie are happy with the spirits in their house. Just after the investigation, Ted left for two weeks to visit his father in Michigan. Debbie didn't mind staying there alone. Both are continuing to learn about ghosts and ghost hunting. So, if the spirits get too active, they will be ready.

Photos by Dan Terry

Richard and Rebecca' Ruediger's 1892 Victorian home sports a period garden and harbors ghosts.

7

504 Mozart

a home filled with good spirits

Rebecca Ruediger had wanted a Victorian home since childhood. Upon the death of her husband's Aunt Laura, she and Richard moved into Laura's house in Hermann. Richard and Rebecca had been living in the Gulf Coast region, where winters are warm and short-sleeved clothing is usually sufficient. Moving to Hermann, where winters are cold, was quite a change for them.

The Ruedigers didn't know what awaited them. His Aunt Laura had lived in the historic Victorian house for 70 years. It had been built in 1892 by Dr. Haeffner, who had the house built to accommodate both his family and his medical practice. It included an office suite with a waiting room and examination room. In 1905, the house had been sold to Theodore and Christine Graff, who lived there with their son, Guy, who eventually married Laura. The Graff family ran a local newspaper. Guy Graff was an attorney and had served as Gasconade County Prosecuting Attorney. After Guy's death, Laura lived in the house for over 50 years. Her only company was a woman who lived in the former doctor's office which had been converted to an apartment.

After a lot of work, the old house was restored to look

the way all Victorian homes should look, but so seldom do. Using Sherwin-Williams Heritage paints in actual Victorian colors and following Rebecca's designer eye, the tan walls and light green decorative gables compete for attention from the street with the tall, silver finials, metal spikes reaching to the clouds.

Richard works on the rose garden, taking up much of the front yard with the old-style varieties of flowers. Other than ripping out the original holly trees, which had been personal favorites of his aunt's as they guarded the front door, he made few changes. The house, with its beautiful garden, reminds one of the glory days of Victorian homes.

For accent, the lights on either side of the front door were salvaged from a horse-drawn hearse that had once belonged to Richard's grandfather, who was the first licensed embalmer in the county. The lights were converted from gas to electric and still illuminate the way for nighttime visitors.

Inside, the hardwood floors are still covered with a Victorian-style carpet Monsanto installed for Aunt Laura in the middle of the 20th century. She had allowed Monsanto to use the home for many of their print ads and, in exchange, they agreed to provide the quality period rug. Just inside the parlor, an Italian marble fireplace gives the room a warm yet sophisticated look.

Rebecca and Richard spent their first night in their "new" home on December 13, 2002, which was Friday the 13th. The Gulf Coast girl was not ready for the cold winds and drafty windows of the 110-year-old building. Nor was she quite ready for the unseen guests who have remained.

"I could hear walking and talking," Rebecca said. "I could often hear conversations between two people but could not make out any words. Just two people talking."

The floors creak loudly as you walk across them. Rebecca can hear the floors creak throughout the house as if someone is walking around while she is home. More than once, she's yelled out, "Who's there?", when she's heard the low conversations or the walking. Now, she just takes it for granted.

Once, a family friend from Houston, Texas, their former Methodist minister and his wife, came for a visit. As the minister climbed up the creaking stairway, he commented, "Your house is filled with good spirits."

Richard, Rebecca and their cats live with the spirits in the house. Whether it's a relative, or a former patient of the doctor who had lived there at the turn of the last century, or a former resident of the house, they keep to themselves. Whoever they are, they seem to be happy with the way the Ruedigers are restoring the old home they loved so well.

Photo by Dan Terry

Zimmer Mit Fruhstuck, "Bed and Breakfast", where you may awaken to the delightful odor of a ghostly breakfast.

8

Zimmer Mit Fruhstuck

where the ghosts make their own breakfast

Gary and Phyllis Craig worked in Washington D.C. for many years. While traveling to Gary's home state of Kansas, they often saw the sign for Hermann along the highway. One day, they decided to stop.

Gary and Phyllis immediately fell in love with the European-style buildings, and with the homes that were similar to those in New England towns. In time, they decided to buy one when they retired. A deal came up three years before they could retire, but the home was so pretty, they decided to purchase it anyway. This would be the home they would never leave.

Apparently, they are not the only residents who feel that way about the house.

Today, Gary and Phyllis run the Zimmer Mit Fruhstuck, which is actually German for "Bed and Breakfast." They also share their home with a spirit—a ghost with some interesting quirks.

"It's never frightening—never scary," Gary said. "It's just something we get used to."

The house was purchased in 1994. The home has two floors, and a stairway just inside the front door connects the two. There is also a stairway outside to the guest room. When the house was built, there was a kitchen on each floor.

It was built by John Bohlken, a local shipbuilder. A check of newspapers from the early twentieth century shows that Bohlken was quite well known, as even his fishing trips made news. In January 1911, he was elected to the board of directors for the Hermann Ferry and Packet Company, sealing his fortune. The house was built in the late Queen Anne style. We know that he did not always live there, as in May 1911, he rented the house to Mr. Quibbert, who became the head miller at the Hermann Star Mill after moving to Hermann from Alton, Illinois.

Gary has been unable to dig up much history on the house. According to legend, a rabies-infected dog was, reportedly, killed on the front porch, but Gary is unsure if it was a stray or a house pet.

While waiting for retirement, Gary and Phyllis had the interior stairway walled off, leaving only the outside entrance to the second floor. They planned to use the upper level as their home-away-from-home, and rent out the lower floor.

The main level was rented to two separate families. Both had the same stories to tell. Upstairs, someone was walking around. A check of the second floor, through the door, showed no one had entered. Yet, nearly every week, the sound of footsteps was heard through the ceiling, disturbing their peace.

Both families complained of hearing the sound of a large animal, such as a dog, walking up in the inaccessible area. They could hear the clicking of its claws on the hardwood floor. Gary said they never found any evidence of an animal having been up in that section.

But the strangest phenomenon was the odor of bacon and eggs cooking. Both families living there, as well as their guests, reported detecting the odor of the phantom breakfast.

In August 1999, Gary and Phyllis moved into their home along with their granddaughter, Laurel. Almost immediately, they noticed the spirits they had been told about.

One morning, while Gary was the only one in the house, he heard loud snoring coming from another bedroom. Quiet as a cat, he slipped down the hallway to catch the trespasser. As Gary opened the door, he was shocked.

The room was empty. Completely empty. Yet, the snoring continued. Sounding like an electric sander with asthma, the noise continued while he stood in the doorway, searching for the source.

His invisible guest was undisturbed.

Later that day, Gary managed to broach the subject with his wife. To his surprise, she had also heard the phantom sleeper snoring away. Phyllis had looked for the source of the sound and not found anyone. She called Laurel into the room. Laurel confirmed having heard the sound as well, but had not told anyone because she could not determine where it was coming from.

Shortly after that, Gary and his granddaughter were watching television in a darkened room. Laurel elbowed Gary, telling him to wake up because he was making too much noise. Gary told her he was awake, and it was not his snoring she was hearing. Apparently, the spirit had sat down with them to watch TV and had dozed off. Finally, they had to turn the volume up to drown out the snores!

In 2005, a couple visiting Hermann stayed at the Zimmer Mit Fruhstuck. It was a pleasant fall evening, and they sat on the front porch. Little did they know what the streets of Hermann had waiting for them.

One noticed that an apparition, visible only from the waist up, was leaning on the house across the street. It was a whitish, misty male form, casually leaning against the corner of the neighbor's house. Both watched as the spirit suddenly straightened and drifted quickly across the street, disappearing near the corner of the house. "And," Gary was quick to add, "neither of them was drinking . . . not a drop!"

But one member of Gary's family was a non-believer. His uncle came for a visit and made jokes about the family's belief in their invisible roommate. That would end when the spirit tired of being the brunt of his jokes.

"First, he noticed the dome light was on inside his car," Gary reported. "My uncle went outside and shut the light off, then locked the door. When he came back inside, he looked out and saw that, once again, the dome light was on." Gary's uncle checked his pockets for the key, then the doors, finding them locked. Once again, he shut off the dome light and locked the doors.

A total of three times, the dome light turned itself on, forcing the skeptic to go outside. Still, he wasn't ready to admit the possibility of a playful specter . . . until 3 A.M., when the radio in his room screamed to life, blaring out a sermon from a religious station they had not programmed.

Gary said that if it had been a clock radio or a remote-controlled radio, he might have shrugged it off. Instead, it was an old-fashioned radio with only a manual control that had been turned on by unseen hands to remind the skeptic uncle that he hadn't been forgotten.

Before Gary's retirement, on one of his frequent trips to his new home, he noticed one of the black window screens was ripped. He went to pick up a new one but could only find gray screen wire. Thinking he would fix it temporarily, Gary left the gray screen on the table in his upstairs apartment until the next day.

The next day, he discovered the screen was gone. No one had been inside the apartment, and nothing else was missing. He decided that the ghost preferred black screens. On his next trip, he replaced it with a black screen. To this day, the gray one has never been found.

Zimmer Mit Fruhstruck is located at 127 W. Third Street, just one block from Market Street and the downtown area, within easy walking distance of the bars, shops and both Stone Hill and Hermannhoff wineries. Enjoy a stay and some friendly conversation with Gary and Phyllis.

But don't make fun of the ghosts.

The ghosts of the tribe
Crouch in the nights
Beside the ghost of a fire.
They try to remember the sunlight,
Light has died out of their skies.
                              —Robinson Jeffers,
                              Apology for Bad Dreams

57

Photo by Dan Terry
Once known as the Central Hotel and Saloon, The Heidelberg was the scene of an 1885 murder.

9

The Heidelberg

a lively little bar . . . for the dead

It wasn't always a saloon. In 1851, William Klee immigrated from Bavaria to Hermann. He worked hard, and eventually purchased a patch of land on Market Street. In 1876, he built his home and set up a small shop, making shoes.

In 1887, Klee took a mortgage on the building, added another floor, and built a smokehouse. Whether due to economics or simply the urge to move on, he sold the building in 1889 to Charles Kimmel.

Apparently, Klee had also opened a bar on the premises. Charles Kimmel was working as a bartender there in 1885 when two of the fine citizens of Hermann put an end to their year-long feud.

According to period newspapers, no one knew the cause of the original fight. What they did know was that Henry Honeck Jr., the local blacksmith, had an ongoing feud with a local tailor, Herman Schlender, who was regarded as an upstanding citizen. The two men had met while skating earlier that day and there had been no problems. But on this Sunday evening in December 1885, for some reason, their argument would come to a conclusion. It had almost ended a month earlier, when the two intoxicated men and their friends were drinking at the Depot Saloon. Without warning, Schlender had grabbed a wine bottle by the neck and swung it at Honeck, cutting his face severely. Neither man reported the incident to the police, but the hatred continued to fester.

It was 11:30 P.M. Schlender was drinking in the saloon at the Central Hotel. Charles Kimmel was tending the bar. Henry Honeck's brother, Edward, ordered a drink. Suddenly, Henry burst through the door and assaulted Schlender. A clothing store proprietor, Schlender was no match for the powerful blacksmith. Honeck had the smaller man almost to the floor when Schlender pulled a pistol and fired point blank into Honeck's chest.

Schlender got free of the clinch and ran out the door. Mortally wounded, Honeck attempted to follow his assassin. However, before he got to the door, he pulled up his shirt, examined his wound, and said to the spectators, "I am shot. I'm dying. Goodbye, Friends." Honeck was dragged to the pool table where he passed away some 15 minutes later.

Schlender was reported to have been seen in Berger, Etlah, and New Haven. However, he was never captured. Public opinion held the sheriff responsible for his escape. So hard was the effect, that the sheriff took out a full-page ad describing his attempts to capture the suspect. It was later determined that Schlender had made it to Sullivan, where he boarded a Frisco train for the Indian Territory (Oklahoma). The *Herman Advertiser-Courier* of December 9, 1885 noted that, "Sheriff Hueller and Detective Mumbrauer last Sunday returned from a long, but fruitless chase after Herman Schlender, the slayer of Henry Honeck, Jr. Schlender eluded his pursuers with much ingenuity, always taking through fields in a zig-zag way. He boarded a Frisco train at Sullivan and has no doubt made his way to the Indian Nation."

In 1889, Charles Kimmel purchased the building, continuing to operate it as the Central Hotel and Saloon. In 1903, Emil Nagel bought the saloon business and, in 1905, purchased the building and began operating the Central Hotel and Saloon as well. Emil was an interesting character in local history. One article in the local paper proclaimed his marriage announcement as such:

As a result of love-making, Mr. Emil Nagel, the saloon man, and

*Miss Leda Emo were last Wednesday quietly married, very few
people in town knowing anything about it until Emil had become
benedict. The young couple is very much in earnest about making
married life a success and if anybody can do so, they can.*

The building passed through various hands and names, most
recently the Heidelberg. It was a bar and restaurant specializing in
"American and German Cuisine", a necessary menu in this proud
German community. The Heidelberg closed a few years ago, and
the building was purchased by the same group that owns the Wine
Valley Inn today.

Employees say the building makes them uncomfortable. At
their request, we went in to investigate. Tim Clifton assisted, along
with Theresa Reavey, new investigator Sherri Missey, and Mike
Greeley. Jeanie Schultz and her husband, Phil, came over from the
Wine Valley Inn to let us into the basement so we could get started.

Immediately Theresa photographed what appeared to be a
blob of colored light, like an orb but blurred. She detected a male
spirit and Tim acquiesced. However, both felt very much at ease
in the damp, dank basement. Theresa believed the spirit there was
friendly and curious, not at all harmful or hateful toward us.

We went to the main floor above. I had explained the
history of the building, leaving out the details of the shooting, the
fight, and any names. I only mentioned the shoemaker's shop, hotel
and saloon. As we went to the back area, both Tim and Theresa
stopped, feeling anger. In one small room to the side, its walls
covered with posters of baseball legends, both said they had seen a
man dressed in overalls, lying on the floor. Theresa said she felt an
argument had transpired, a long, drawn-out fight, before one of the
men was injured. Neither Tim nor Theresa believed the man had
died there, only that he had lain there injured upon the floor.

I walked in to share my findings with Jeanie, to show her
how accurate the sensitives had been. I was quickly called back into
the room. Tim, Sherri, and Mike had all heard a voice speak in their
ears in separate incidents. None could make out a word, only the
sound of someone speaking very close to their heads, as if sharing a
secret.

After a little more time, we proceeded upstairs. On the

second floor, which had been converted from hotel rooms into one large apartment, clothing and blankets lay strewn around the room. Beds, TVs, and furniture had been left behind by the previous tenants, who had been gone at least three years. Jeanie informed us that prior to the closing of the restaurant and bar, this space had been rented out to illegal immigrants from Mexico, all of whom suddenly disappeared after harvest season.

Finding very little there, we proceeded to the final level, the third floor. There, both sensitives believed they felt the presence of a woman in torment. Possibly a miscarriage or an abortion was responsible for her feelings of guilt. At that time, only the KII meter showed any signs of the spirits, and it was shaky at best. Since the temperature was 93 degrees upstairs, we quickly decided to go back downstairs to take a break.

After some time, we went back to the first floor and hooked up the Ovilus. I began speaking to the spirits, asking who was present. For several minutes, nothing came up. In fact, someone mentioned that the Ovilus was much quieter than usual. We asked about soldiers, the Civil War, the Depression, and even World War II, with no results.

I asked about Emil Nagel's marriage, making some unflattering remarks about his wife. The Ovilus began speaking, saying words such as "property" and "home". I then began talking about Henry. The Ovilus suddenly spoke the word "shot."

Believing I was talking to Henry Honeck, I began to ask questions about his death. The Ovilus became quiet. I asked about Schlender, and the word, "Ran" issued forth. I even quoted the last words Henry Honeck Jr., uttered as he lay dying on the pool table. The Ovilus replied immediately with the word "Shot" once again.

Tim believed that we were not speaking with either participant in the events of that dreadful day, but with a spirit leading us down a false path. He and Theresa both believed we should return to the third floor of the building.

Once upstairs, I set up the Ovilus. It did not go off after the first few words spoken as it took the readings of the new room so it was fairly useless. What did happen was a little less technological, but just as startling.

Tim and Theresa began to attempt contact with the female

spirit. Tim got the image of what he believed to be a circus or carnival, with brightly-colored tents and animals in cages. The overriding emotion was one of guilt. Tim believed the spirit was cowering on the floor behind me. I kneeled down and placed the Ovilus there. A photo taken by Sherri showed a large orb at that exact location.

Phil said he felt cold. The ambient temperature of the room was still over 90 degrees. Again, he said he felt cold. I walked over to him, placing my hand on his shoulder. While there were no fans, open windows, or electricity in this part of the building, his shoulder seemed to be at least twenty degrees cooler than the room. I mentioned that he was freezing.

He quickly warmed up. Tim believed the spirit had gone into the next room, so I followed. Again, I felt what seemed to be a twenty-degree difference in the room. It warmed up when the ghost moved. At least two other investigators felt the coolness of the spirit as it moved away from us, finally leaving the room altogether.

We locked the Heidelberg up for the night. There had only been limited access by humans for several years, and whatever spirits remained seemed weak. We'll attempt it again and see if the ghosts of the past are more talkative later.

Photos by Dan Terry

*Above: Hermann
Cemetery
Left: The "Witch's
Stone"*

10

Hermann City Cemetery

a graveyard straight from a vampire novel

ven in broad daylight, the old Hermann Cemetery on the
crown of the hill at Ninth Street is spooky. At the top of the
graveyard, several stones are five- to seven-feet high. Rusting
wrought-iron fences surround many of the graves, with fence parts
missing, a reminder of the metal shortages in World War II as well as
the acts of vandals. Many of these white monuments are broken and
others lean at odd angles, as if the ground has grown tired of holding
them up. The dates go back to the mid-1800's, a testimony to the
perseverance of the German settlers.

At night, one may expect to see zombies walking between
the stones. The old cemetery resembles a backdrop from a Victorian-
style vampire or werewolf movie. The full moon reflecting off the
broken and falling stones on the steep hill will have the brave
traveler looking over his shoulder as much as at his feet, where the
shattered stones wait to trip him.

Three stones here are specifically worth mentioning. At the
top of the hill, to the south, is George Bayer's grave. Long ignored
because of the edict that no one would be buried within 75 feet of

his grave, a group of citizens several years ago held a court within the city of Hermann, where they heard the trials and tribulations of the founder of the city. It was decided at that time that the much-maligned deputy had been given far more tasks than any one man could reasonably be expected to do, and he was exonerated. Today, his stone displays the original German language epitaph with an English translation on a metal plaque next to it. A fence surrounds the monument as a tribute to the man who helped create Hermann, the city that lies within the panoramic view below the graveyard.

Nearby stands a monument to the victims of the *Big Hatchie* riverboat disaster. Over 35 unclaimed bodies are buried in a mass grave below it. While the stone bears the incorrect date of the disaster, the sentiment is admirable.

Between these two stones lies a true mystery. Sitting alone, an impressive four-foot tall stone is endowed with the most amazingly-intricate skull and crossbones ever seen. The name and dates have been lost to time and the elements. Early records of the dead were listed by name, not by grave location, thereby providing no enlightenment. On the left and right sides of the stone are two more skull-and-crossbones carvings, apparently holding back drapes. The design, still evil-looking after all these years, leaves one with a morbid touch of respect for the artist.

Area legends differ on the reason for the stone. One theory indicates that it is a symbol of a high-ranking member of the Independent Order of Odd Fellows, a benevolent group started in the United States in 1819. Another local legend says buried treasure was placed beneath this stone. A third would have us believe that the symbol was used to warn potential grave robbers that the person buried there had died from a highly-contagious disease.

But local youngsters have the most entertaining legend of the skull stone. They believe the stone marks the last resting place of a witch, who was killed in the mid-1800's by the very religious and superstitious German immigrants. They say that if you touch the stone, you will have bad luck within 24 hours. This legend gives the grave an unholy fascination to the local kids as well as to local ghost hunters.

I can personally relate this story: In 2004, I was writing my first newspaper story on local ghosts and went to photograph the famed witch's stone. I parked near the top of the hill, put fresh batteries into the camera, batteries I had just purchased from Wal-Mart the day before, then I approached the marker.

A large ebony crow flew in and landed on the stone just as I approached it. Everyone knows that black crows and black cats are considered witches' familiars. The non-reflective eyes and shiny black feathers give these large birds an evil look in their own right. Knowing this would be an outstanding photograph, I raised the camera slowly and attempted to take the photo.

Nothing. The batteries were completely drained. I had checked to see that they were fully charged before leaving the truck. Now the camera was useless, and the crow seemed to be laughing at me.

I purchased new batteries at a local convenience store, and returned to the graveyard. Of course, the crow was gone and the camera worked perfectly. I probably just purchased a bad set of batteries, which just happened to go dead as I was attempting to photograph a reputed witch's grave while a black bird chanced to land on it. Just my bad luck. Maybe.

Once, while I was there with Tim Clifton, he distinctly heard a female voice say, "Hello." Tim was standing near a concrete wall surrounding a few stones with a steep drop-off on the downhill side. The same area, in fact, I would return to later to get a photograph for the cover of this book.

On that trip, I placed a wine glass on the wall, and took the photo while lying across two graves. This allowed me to focus on the wine glass, making the leaning, gothic-like stones in the background seem out of focus. Later, while going over the photos, Sherri discovered what seemed to be a reflection in the glass just above the wine level. A man's face appeared, frowning, and apparently wearing a suit. Sherri and I were the only ones in the entire cemetery that day. It seemed that the man was unhappy, possibly because I was lying across his final resting place.

Next time I go to that cemetery, I'll apologize profusely.

Photo by Dan Terry

Note the detail shown in the inset enlargement from this glass of wine photographed at the Hermann Cemetery. A man's face appears. He is apparently wearing a suit. Perhaps he was unhappy because Dan stretched out across his "final" resting place to take the photo.

As a duly designated representative of the City, County and State of New York, I order you to cease any and all supernatural activity and return forthwith to your place of origin or to the nearest convenient parallel dimension.

—Ghostbusters, 1984

Photos by Dan Terry

OakGlenn Winery where a noisy ghost continues to make his presence known

11

OakGlenn Winery

beautiful scenery and a noisy ghost

When Glenn and Carol Warnebold first saw their new farm, Carol fell in love immediately with the area. The gentle, sloping hills overlooked the Missouri River. Once a thriving winery, this little retirement farm would soon be producing 5,000 to 10,000 gallons of wine again.

According to the owners of OakGlenn Winery, the area was once called "Schau-ins-land" meaning "a look into the country". This name came from its incredible view of the Missouri River and surrounding river valley. It was originally owned by George Husmann, a well-known horticulturist and wine maker.

Husmann was born November 4, 1827, in Europe. His father had bought shares in the colony that was being set up by the German Settlement Society of Philadelphia. In 1847, Husmann started a grape farm outside Hermann, as did many of the other settlers, who found the land too steep and rocky for much else.

After serving in the Civil War with the Union forces, Husmann was sent to the State Constitutional Convention, drafting *An Ordinance Abolishing Slavery in Missouri*. It was the first such law to be enacted in the United States.

He wrote a book entitled, *The Cultivation of Native Grapes and Manufacture of American Wine,* which would become a textbook for American wine makers. He also created a publication called *The American Grape Grower.* In 1870, Husmann was appointed to the Board of Curators for the University of Missouri. Not bad for a self-educated man! He later helped direct James Simonton in creating a root stock resistant to Phylloxera, a disease of grape vines. The disease so destroyed the crops of France that Husmann sent millions of the disease-resistant root stocks from Hermann and surrounding areas so French farmers could graft them to their bordeau vines. This graft process enabled the bordeau vine to become productive once again, saving the wine-making industry in that country. Today, two monuments stand in France in honor of Missouri winemakers for assisting in the rescue of that valuable French resource.

George Husmann died in 1902 at the age of 75. However, Carol still feels his presence in the wine cellar where he tended the bottles over 140 years ago. And she attributes the feeling of warmth and welcome she feels there to this presence, a belief reinforced by the abnormal number of strongly-glowing orbs that have been photographed by visitors. Possibly one reason for his remaining there is that the same vines he planted long ago are again producing Norton wine, now crafted into the OakGlenn Red Port.

After the Husmann family, the farm was owned by a family named Loehnig, who saw more tragedy than the Husmann family had experienced. In 1872, 40-year-old Theresa, who was the wife and mother of the family, fell from a chair where she had been standing while trimming the tree on Christmas Eve. Pregnant, she bled to death the next day. Another member of the family was found dead in the barn, which has since been converted to a bedroom in the house. While clearing the hill, Carol and Glenn found the historic Loehnig family cemetery, from which they removed considerable brush and debris. They fenced in the cemetery and placed a large wooden cross there, a cross that had been made by a local priest.

The wine cellar, dug out in 1859, is believed to have been a station in the underground railroad, with runaway slaves coming up the Missouri River, staying for a short time, then moving on up the river to Alton, Illinois, and on to Chicago and freedom.

The hill near the cellar was covered with large rocks, which Carol often threw off into the woods. The previous owner was visiting, and asked what happened to them. When she explained, the visitor said he had been told this had something to do with a sacred Indian site, possibly a burial area. He offered no further enlightenment.

When Carol and Glenn purchased the property, the stone walls of the house/barn combination were still in pretty good shape, but weeds grew inside the house. Everything was gutted and rebuilt, with a bedroom placed in the area that was once part of the barn. One night, Carol was awakened by what sounded like metal pipes being banged together. The horrendous racket failed to awaken either Glenn or the family dog. Carol said the cacophony continued for as much as five minutes before finally stopping. Glenn apparently heard nothing. In time, Carol put it out of her mind.

Then, in 2006, a nephew staying with them in that room reported the same thing, having never heard Carol's story. He complained that in the night, a loud ruckus of what sounded like someone banging on metal pipes with a wrench woke him up from a sound sleep. The banging continued for several minutes before stopping. Interestingly enough, there are not now, nor have there ever been, metal pipes in that area of the house! There is also a persistent foul odor in the closet that will not disappear no matter what Carol does to eliminate it.

For the photographer, no stop in Hermann is complete without a stop at OakGlenn and a photo of the Missouri River as it winds around the hills and bluffs. And for the ghost story lover, a few minutes of talking to Carol or Glenn will send shivers down your spine that only a glass of smooth wine can settle. Enjoy!

Photo by Dan Terry

Above: 2009 Wharf Street Scene

Below: Old photo of three unidentified ladies enjoying the scenery at the Hermann waterfront in bygone days.

conclusion

These Are But a Few . . .

While I am aware that there are plenty more ghosts and ghost stories in Hermann than I have related here, we must bring this set of adventures to a close.

Why is Hermann so haunted? For the same reasons that St. Charles, Alton, Illinois, St. Louis, Hannibal, and a host of other river cities are haunted. A combination of the extensive history, the moving water which generates energy that the spirits can tap into, and the limestone bedrock that seems to hold the psychic energy. My own belief is that the long, sometimes painful history associated with places like Hermann cause such numerous hauntings.

Leaving Hermann for now, there are a few places I would like to get back to and investigate. Here are a few:

1. The Gasconade County Courthouse: Dedicated in July 1898, it is believed to be one of the only courthouses in the nation built entirely by private funds. Charles Eitzen, a self-made millionaire, willed the county $50,000 to build a courthouse replacing a much smaller brick building. To make the bricks shine, they were rubbed with beer rather than the usual vinegar, because in Hermann the beer was cheaper. It has been the scene of a fire, an abduction that ended with a lynching, a legal hanging, and at least one suicide.

When I was a street cop working in Owensville, the dispatchers who worked for the Gasconade County Sheriff's Department told me often of hearing voices and footsteps in the hallway, but finding no one on the monitors. Many refused to leave the well-lit dispatch center at night. When I spoke to an employee recently, she proclaimed "Oh, yes. We have a ghost."

2. The Showboat Theater: Originally built in 1934, this building shared a common wall with a well-established bar. It was named the "Hermo" during a contest won by a schoolboy who combined the words, "Hermann" and "Missouri". It has operated on and off since then. The structure fell into disrepair and the owner left. It was taken over by a local bank and donated to a not-for-profit group called Historic Hermann, Inc. Today, the theater hosts plays and concerts several times a year.

Theaters are notorious for being haunted, and unsubstantiated rumors abound regarding this one—lights going on and off—ghostly actors being seen around the theater.

3. The White House: A former hotel and apartment building, it is presently the home of a bed and breakfast. Several occupants from the apartment days tell of moving mists, ghostly people walking down the stairs, the sound of someone walking the halls, etc. It was the scene of at least two suicides. A woman disappeared on Wharf Street leaving behind her very expensive clothes and belongings. The current owners claim, on their web site, that the only ghost there is the Holy Ghost. However, they do confirm that their guests have made occasional reports of paranormal activity.

4. Sharp's Corner Bar: This long-running establishment has the best burgers in the county—just a little greasy and peppery, but the fries are great! Other than Maifest and Octoberfest, Sharp's is mostly a locals' hangout. Rumor has it that an old man who used to come in daily for a beer can still be seen on occasion, years after his death, sitting on his favorite stool and enjoying his favorite drink.

5. Stone Hill Winery: The huge, hand-dug wine cellars are the scene of reported paranormal activity, possibly by a former employee

who forgot to clock out after death.

6. The Wholt House B and B: It was built by August Wholt, a shipbuilder who served as the first mayor of Hermann. Current guests claim to hear footsteps walking up and down the stairs and objects being moved.

7. Hermannhof Winery: Completed in 1852, this winery began as a brewery and a small winery, with the wine business eventually growing into its main concern. I had heard from several people that the winery was haunted. I went in to speak with the manager, who was on vacation. However a clerk, after I related the purpose of my visit, said, "Oh, yeah. You need to speak with him. It's haunted." I shall return.

8. The Concert Hall and Barrel Bar: Until the mid 1990's when the business was closed for a major restoration, this bar was, reportedly, the oldest bar west of the Mississippi in continuous operation. It was here that a fight started that ended with the shooting death of the town blacksmith at the Heidelberg. I've heard no rumors, and the current owners have yet to hold a grand opening, but I'll keep on it.

Many private homes are reportedly haunted, but the living residents are content with their paranormal lodgers, and still tend not to speak of the spirits. But the area is filled with ghostly reminders of the past, both long ago and recent. And it all makes Hermann, Missouri, a great getaway for the wine lover, beer taster, sausage fan or the ghost hunter.

Links for Further Exploration

Haunted Bed and Breakfast in Hermann
   The Wine Valley Inn   www.wine-valley-inn.com
   Zimmer Mit Fruhstuck www.zimmerhermann.com

Wineries:
   OakGlenn Winery   www.oakglenn.com
   Hermannhof Winery www.hermannhof.com
   Stone Hill Winery   www.stonehillwinery.com

For Paranormal Help or Advice:

Greg Myers: greg@paranormaltaskforce.com
Steven LaChance: steven@stevenalachance.com
Dr. Michael Henry: info@stcharlesghosttours.com
S.I.: www.supernaturalinvestigations.com

Author's web site:
Dan Terry: www.spookstalker.com

Publisher's web site:
missourikidpress.com

Other Dan Terry Books Offered by Missouri Kid Press
(Actual Covers are Printed in Color)

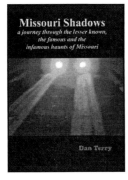

Missouri Shadows: A Journey Through the Lesser Known, the Famous and the Infamous Haunts of Missouri
by Dan Terry   Soft Cover - 6 x 9 - 182 pps
Author Dan Terry continues to bring his police background into play to search out the paranormal, utilizing police techniques and scientific equipment. In this book, Terry explores the paranormal in various Missouri locations. Mark A. Mihalko, editor of *Haunted Times Magazine,* said, "The stories inside are full of atmosphere, perfect for those brisk windy nights where every sound is magnified by the silence!
$14.99 ($15.89 including Mo. Sales Tax) + $3 shipping

Beyond the Shadows: Exploring the Ghosts of Franklin County
by Dan Terry   Soft Cover - 6 x 9 - 51 pps
Author Dan Terry brings his police background into play to search out the paranormal, utilizing police techniques and scientific equipment. In this book, Terry explores the paranormal in various Franklin County, Missouri locations, including the Harney Mansion, Enoch's Knob Bridge, The Diamonds, and sites in New Haven and Berger, Missouri. Extreme Haunting Specialist Steven LaChance said, "Lock your doors and take a fun, but terrifying journey with Spookstalker Dan into the unknown".
$12.00 ($12.72 including Mo. Sales Tax) + $3 shipping

To order additional copies of this book, see pages 80 and 82.

BE SURE to specify WHICH BOOK you are ordering!

Missouri Kid Press, P. O. Box 111, Stanton, Missouri 63079
573-927-2772 missourikidpress@hotmail.com

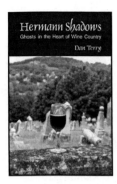

Hermann Shadows: Exploring the Ghosts of
Franklin County
by Dan Terry   Soft Cover - 6 x 9 - 90 pps
Author Dan Terry again utilizes his police background to
search out the paranormal. Michael Henry, Ph.D., writes,
"Dan is a meticulous researcher and an entertaining
storyteller. Together, let's explore a few of the ghosts
in Hermann, Missouri, another of those wonderful
intriguing, haunted places." He added, "Sound travels
here and spirits travel here [Hermann]. Perhaps these two
energies follow the same paths."

To order more copies of the book you are holding, send
$12.99 ($13.77 including Mo. Sales Tax) + $3 shipping

A History of Moselle, Missouri
(exact title to be determined)
by Sue Blesi
This town, situated east of St. Clair in Franklin
County, Missouri, was once a picturesque river
town and a growing center of commerce. Hustle
and bustle filled the air as livestock, gravel, rails,
brooms, tobacco, and other products were staged for
shipping on the Frisco. The village disincorporated
years ago and, today, there are no businesses
or industries. Soft Cover. Size 8 x 10 in. To be
Published Fall 2009

**COMING
SOON from
Missouri Kid
Press**

At Our Wit's End: Our Speech Has Roots in the
Wisdom Books
by Glen Blesi
We are often unaware of the Biblically-based
phrases we use in our everyday conversation. To be
published Winter 2009

Other Books Offered by Missouri Kid Press
(Actual Covers are Printed in Color)

Where Dead Men Still Fight: a History of Stanton, Missouri
by Sue Blesi   Soft Cover - 8 x 10 in - 402 pps
A history of Stanton, Missouri, and the neighboring communities of Reedville and Anaconda. Expounds on the lives of pioneer settlers, including John Stanton, and the men the streets were named for. Includes the post office, businesses, churches, schools, history of Meramec Caverns, the Missouri Kid, Route 66, as well as information on the people, places and events in Stanton and burials in the Stanton, Anaconda, Hendrix and Rock Hill cemeteries. Over-sized book with lots of photographs.
   Price $32.99 ($34.96 including Mo. Sales Tax) + $5 Priority Shipping

Ordering Information

Mail to: Missouri Kid Press
Post Office Box 111
Stanton, Missouri 63079

or

email: missourikidpress@hotmail.com

*Note: Price, taxes, and shipping subject to change

Provide us with your name, mailing address, including city, state and zip code. We need a telephone number or email address in case there are questions about your order.

List the titles of the books you wish to order, along with the sales tax (Missouri residents only) and shipping charge.

Please verify current price with publisher prior to ordering and BE SURE to specify WHICH BOOK(s) you are ordering.

NOTE: Special pricing and shipping reduction available for 12 or more copies of the same title to one address. Contact publisher for specifics.

Payment can be in the form of a money order, personal check or certified check, sent to the above-listed mailing address. Publisher has the right to hold checks until they clear before mailing books.

Books are sent by First Class Mail unless otherwise specified.

These books are also available on Amazon.com.